TALK SENSE!

by Sammy Horner

CHRISTIAN FOCUS PUBLICATIONS

WHAT'S INSIDE...

TIME FOR A CHECK UP!

GROW UP!

START HERE!

Our bodies are amazing! Have you ever wondered how they work?What keeps us alive, makes us think, or laugh? Why do our bodies get sick or stop working? Did you know there is one specialist Doctor who is very interested in you? He wants to make sure you're healthy and in good shape. Read on and find out if you're as fit as you thought...

Published by Christian Focus Publications Ltd Geanies House, Tain, Ross-shire, IV20 1TW
©1997 Sammy Horner reprinted 2002 Previously published as Time for a Check up and Grow up now published as Talk Sense in one volume Illustrations by Tim Charnick, Profile Design ISBN 1-85792-757-5
www.christianfocus.com

'DOCTOR, DOCTOR, I FEEL LIKE A PAIR OF CURTAINS'

How many corny 'Doctor doctor' jokes have you heard? You know the kind...

'Doctor, doctor, I feel like a snooker ball'...
'Well, get to the end of the queue!' or
'Doctor, doctor, people keep ignoring me'...
'Next!'

Oh dear...bad jokes about doctors seem to be endless, but how would you feel if your doctor really said those things? The fact is that doctors are there to help us get better when we are sick. They are able to deal with all kinds of situations. Doctors do their very best to help us.

Can you imagine what it would be like if doctors just told you to go home and pull yourself together? Things go wrong with people all the time, and it's then that we are glad to have doctors.

- YOU CAN'T PULL YOURSELF TOGETHER

In a book called the Bible, we are told that something has gone wrong with every single person in the whole world. It's not really a disease, but it's very serious and it works in people's minds and bodies, just like an illness.

You won't find this 'illness' described in any medical book, in fact you won't even find the word, but you just need to look at the world around us to see that this problem is everywhere. The Bible calls it, 'sin', a teeny little word that has a big meaning for all of us.

In the same way as an illness shows itself in what doctors call symptoms, (like when your face gets spotty if you catch Chicken Pox!) so the Bible tells us about the symptoms of this worldwide epidemic! You can't always see sin in the same way as you might see the result of a broken arm or a swollen ankle...it affects us in a very different way.

Sin touches every part of us, our body, our mind and our feelings. It affects how we behave, our attitude to other people and even our attitude to God himself. Sin is such a nasty thing that it is the only thing about us that God hates.

The good news is that God loves people, but he sees how sin affects you and is willing to do whatever is necessary to get rid of it! He is like a great doctor who is willing to work with people who need cured...he hates the problem, but he loves the person. The symptoms can be seen in every single person. It seems to be more serious in some people, but every one has got them, and everyone is in need of help.

SYMPTOMS OF SIN
greed
lies
stealing
violence
treating others badly...
selfishness
not caring for people....
being ungrateful...
hatred
gossiping...

Here are some of the symptoms of sin that the Bible mentions... do you have any?

There are even more, but you can see that all of us do some of these things from time to time. The fact is that we can't just pull ourselves together, we need help!

The Bible tells us that God knew all about this problem and decided to do something about it. His plan was incredible, and involved God coming into this world as a man - he was called Jesus.

He wants to help and he can help, no matter how badly sin has damaged you.

HELP FROM A REAL SPECIALIST!

Just about everything that needs fixed has a specialist 'fixer'. We have already said that doctors help fix our bodies, so how come as soon as we find out that there is a problem with every single person in the world we don't go to the best doctor of all? No one else in history has been able to sort out this problem of sin...no one, except Jesus that is!

The thing about doctors is that they understand how people's bodies work and what needs to be done to sort the problem... they know what all the bits do. They understand what makes it tick! The Bible tells us that God made human beings. He knows how our bodies work and he knows what is best for us.

When God became a man, he also understood the kinds of problems that we have as human beings, because he went through them as well. Did you know that Jesus knew what it was like to:

FEEL HUNGRY AND THIRSTY

HAVE FRIENDS DISAPPOINT HIM

FEEL LONELY

FEEL SLEEPY

GET HURT

BE ACCUSED OF THINGS HE DIDN'T DO

AND LOADS OF OTHER THINGS...

He knew what it was like to feel under pressure. Jesus not only knows what we need, but he understands what it's like to live in this world. The really amazing thing about Jesus is that even though he had real pressure put on him to give into sin...he never did.

Jesus is the only person in all history to live without any sin in his life. In the same way that doctors are qualified to treat our illnesses, Jesus is qualified to deal with our problem of sin because of who he is and what he has done.

SICK TO THE BACK TEETH!

So how serious is this problem? How does it affect you? Can you recognise the symptoms in your own life?

The Bible tells us that every single person has certain things about them that reminds us that God made human beings. We feel a certain way if we see other people suffering. Feelings of sympathy, care and being fair all come from God 'cause that's what he is like. Jesus was the most caring, loving, fair minded person who ever lived, and that is how we are meant to be.

Let's take a look at what the Bible says about the parts of us that sin has affected:

You see ***why*** we do things is just as important as doing those good things. Sin causes us trouble in many ways!

Now because you are a sinner doesn't mean that you are completely horrible and slobber n' scream n' rant n' rave!

It does mean however, that you are not everything that God wanted you to be. It means that your relationship with God is damaged and that sin can get a stronger hold on you.
It touches everything that people are involved in. The question is...what are we going to do about it?

4 The Healing Process

Just as the Bible tells us about the symptoms of sin, it also clearly shows us the *only* cure.

Jesus was so concerned about our sins that he showed us how we should live - he also did something incredible!

He knew that our sin stopped us from being friends with God. Jesus was accused of all kinds of terrible things that he wasn't guilty of.

He was called:
a liar, a greedy man,
a drunk, a terrorist,
a fraud, a devil
a man who made friends
with dangerous,
dirty, cheating
and violent people.

Although none of this was true, Jesus was accused and killed on a cross.

This seems like bad news, and in a way it is certainly sad news, but it's also good news. God let his Son Jesus die on the cross. Why?

Jesus was completely innocent and yet he took the punishment for all the bad stuff we have mentioned...and even more! When we become aware of how much God loves us, and all that he has done for us, we start to understand how bad sin is. We begin to see that our sins have been hurting others and offending God.

It's like all the bad stuff anyone has ever done was dealt with by Jesus. So now when a person believes in Jesus, God doesn't accuse or blame them for being greedy or lying, because his own innocent Son died for everyone who has done those things.

JESUS DIED FOR

My Sin

It's a bit like someone else paying a bill for you...you don't have to pay for what you've done wrong in God's sight (although doing wrong things sometimes has consequences for the future). All you have to do is accept what Jesus did for you!

We'll start with the heart!

Gary wasn't a bad lad...just a bit of a joker. He always made fun of *everything*. When the circus had a parade through town Gary made jokes about everything.

Three camels went by in procession, Gary shouted, 'Hi there Humphry... geddit? Hump three!' All the lads laughed.

The clowns came by next. When they were giving out noses, those guys thought that they said 'roses' and asked for really big red ones! Get it?...Roses and noses... The guys giggled!

Later in the supermarket he asked the man behind the counter for a box of Ten o'clock mints. 'Don't you mean *After Eights?*' asked the man. 'Same thing' said Gary, 'ten o'clock is after eight isn't it? Do ya get it? Ten...after eight?' His chums chuckled!

The only time that Gary couldn't make a joke was when *she* was around. She was the cutest girl in the whole solar system. She had short dark hair, always dressed really cool, had a smile that would melt the North Pole...her name was Hazel and so were her eyes! Every time she appeared Gary went all dopey. He got all his words back to front and upside down. 'Happy to see you' became 'Hippy to sneeze you'. 'You're looking rather nice today!' ended up sounding like, 'You're cooking father's rice today!'

'Oh no,' thought Gary as he saw Hazel walking towards him, 'I always sound like such a twit when I try to talk to her... and to make things worse my mates are here!'

Wee Tommy and Colin braced themselves for the biggest laugh of the day...they knew how Gary spoke whenever he saw Hazel.

'C'mon now,' Gary thought to himself. 'How hard can it be to say, 'Hi Hazel...where are you off to?' The words were right in his mind. He rehearsed them over and over as Hazel drew closer and closer, then, just as he was about to speak she went and did it...she smiled at him!

'Hiz... Hizil... pears are soft too! Doooh!' Colin creased in two while Tommy laughed so hard a big bubble appeared out of his nose.

Gary went really red! Hazel ignored the two boys, smiled at Gary and said. 'Youth Club.'

'Youth Club!' said all three lads together. 'Boring!'they yapped. 'It's in the old church hall!'

Gary was just about to tell his daft church joke, 'Why do churches have steeples? So that everyone can see the point!' when he remembered that he'd probably get it wrong while still in the vicinity of the Hazel Zone!

'You can come if you want to,' said Hazel.

Gary wasn't interested in church much...but he was interested in Hazel!

Tommy and Colin laughed and giggled while Gary desperately tried to think of a way to suggest that they follow Hazel to church...and still look cool!

'Let's go for a laugh!' suggested Gary. 'We can make fun of everything at church!'

Tommy and Colin agreed. It wasn't what they expected, lots of people their age, loud music, videos and flashing lights. Between the music and videos, some guy spoke about stuff like faith and Jesus but he didn't speak for very long, so the boys listened. Gary didn't want to look too interested, and so he waited for the best moment to make a wise crack. Hazel was far enough away to stop his words getting twisted, so Gary waited and waited and waited.

'It's important that we allow Jesus to have our heart,' said the between videos guy.

'No thanks !' yelled Gary, 'I don't fancy the operation much!'

Colin nearly choked on his cherry coke, while Tommy's face screwed up so much with laughter that Gary thought that he looked as if he had a fold away head!

Only the three boys laughed, the rest of the room was so quiet that you could have heard a spider burp!

A video burst into life and the programme continued without any more dumb comments.

On the way out, the guy was saying good-bye to everyone at the door. Gary got closer and nervous all at the same time. Just as he reached the door and expected a good telling off, the guy said, 'So you don't fancy the operation then? You think that giving your heart to someone involves surgery, do you?'

'What else could it mean?' asked Gary. 'Everyone knows that your heart is just a pump that squirts blood around your body. It's just a bloodpump!'

Tommy and Colin never made a sound, but their shoulders went up and down .

'And fathermear,' continued Gary, 'hi don't stink bat chew half the write doo smell us fat to chew...errr...to do!' It was happening again...Hazel had to be close. Sure enough, there she was only three feet away.

'Oh no, I'm done for,' thought Gary.

The guy saw Gary's reaction to Hazel and began to speak again.

'Just imagine for a moment that you really liked a girl. Imagine that you and she went for a long romantic walk through a beautiful field of wheat, and then down beside the river!'

Gary got even redder than before. First his neck, then his ears, then his whole head. From a distance, with his white Tee-shirt and big red head, he looked a bit like a match stick! The guy went on.

'As you get down to the river you take a little diamond ring from your pocket, look deep into the girl's big brown eyes...'

Gary glanced at Hazel...he could feel a big drip of sweat dangling from his nose...at least he hoped it was sweat!

'... and just as you are about to put it on her finger she pulls her hand away and says, "Haven't you got anything to say first?"

'With all your might, you think through your most romantic proposal and with all the passion you can muster you say... 'Darling... I really love you with all my bloodpump!'

Everyone laughed, even Gary thought that the guy was pretty funny.

The guy went on, 'You see, to give your heart to someone is a great act of faith. You are saying that you trust that person completely. That you know that they will not hurt you or misuse you.

'Everybody needs their bloodpump heart to live, but to say that we trust someone with our heart, or that we love someone with our heart, or even that we will give our heart to someone really means that we are ready to dedicate ourselves to that person for ever...it means that you are going to give your all to that person...that is how we need to give ourselves to Jesus!'

'I geddit,' said Gary, 'I Geddit!'

Sometimes you may hear other people who believe in Jesus using all kinds of words and expressions that you don't understand. It's OK to ask what they are talking about.

Remember that the story of Jesus is a Love story. It's all about the fact that God loved us **so much** that he was willing to let Jesus give his life to help us understand his love for us.
When you see it like that, it's not surprising that we often use words like, 'Giving our heart to God.' We just mean that we are now devoted to the God who really loves us.

CHECKUP FROM THE NECK UP!

We've already talked about 'the heart', but what about the mind? The things that we think about are really important.

Jesus said that if we...

Then we are keeping the two most important commands in the world!

He said that loving God means using our mind, as well as our emotions, feelings and bodies. It is very important that we use our brain when we decide to do what God says! We use our mind to help us make decisions.

God's ideas on how people should think and behave are often very different to our own ideas. Imagine what the world would be like if people thought the same way as God! Imagine a world in which people loved their enemies.

God wants to help you see people and life in a new way. This new way of thinking may seem strange to other people. It's like a complete turn around from the normal way of life, but God tells us in the Bible that his way is always the best way! To be fair, sympathetic, caring, brave, helpful, loving and kind is more like how

God intended people to be.
An ordinary doctor checks us out to make sure

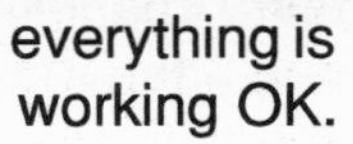

everything is working OK.

We need to allow God to check out what we are watching, listening to, getting involved in and what we are putting into our minds.

God wants to be involved in ***all*** of our life. He may want to change some of it, ask us to do new things that we have never thought about or to be careful about what we say and do.

In the same way as we trust our doctor to get us back in shape, we need to trust God to remove anything that may cause damage or harm.

Breathe Deeply!

7

Every animal in the world breathes...they have to otherwise they wouldn't be alive! People need to breathe as well, but did you know that human beings are not just another animal!

At the very beginning of the Bible in a book called Genesis, we find the story of God's amazing creation. We are told that God gave everything life, but when he made human beings, he did something different. He said that men and women would be made in his image. I don't think that means that God looks like us physically, but rather that he gave us certain things that make us something like him. Do you ever wonder why we feel sad when we watch news reports on TV? Why we cry at pictures of hungry people? Why we want to see people treated fairly and get annoyed when they are not? Well that's how God made us.

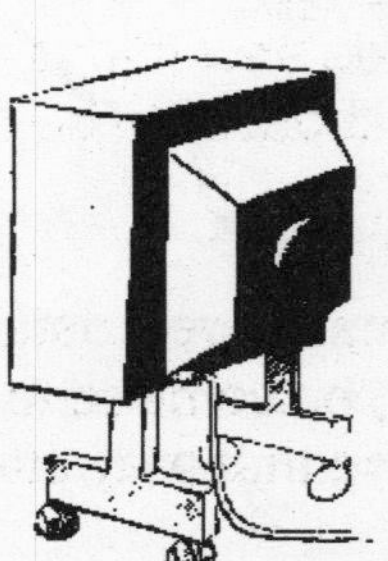

The Bible says that God took great care over his creation, but that he took a special interest in human beings...in fact one part of the story says that God 'breathed life into the man'.

If we want to follow God, we still struggle with sin and do wrong things, but God has promised to help us. When we become a Christian we are filled with God's Holy Spirit. He is there to comfort, guide and teach us throughout our whole life. Having God's Spirit is as important for living as having breath in our lungs.

Although we cannot see the Spirit of God, the Bible promises us that he is with Christians all the time. He helps us to decide what is good or bad. He helps us see life in a new way.

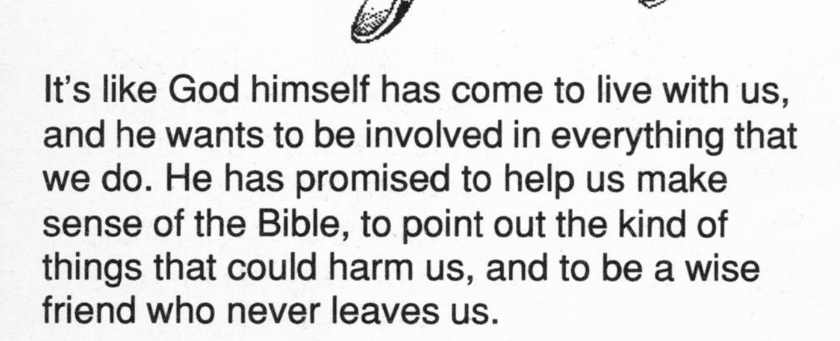

It's like God himself has come to live with us, and he wants to be involved in everything that we do. He has promised to help us make sense of the Bible, to point out the kind of things that could harm us, and to be a wise friend who never leaves us.

STARTING A FULL RECOVERY!

Finding out how much God has done for us can make us feel really great grateful, but it can also make us feel sad that Jesus was treated so badly because of our wrong doing. Understanding these two things is the start of a full recovery.

Being grateful to God and understanding how much he loves you makes him very happy. To hear you say that you are sorry for all the rotten things that you have done is the best and most exciting thing that God ever hears from a person.

Talking to God is called prayer. It's best if you talk to God in your own words and tell him how you feel...that way you know what you mean...and so does God!

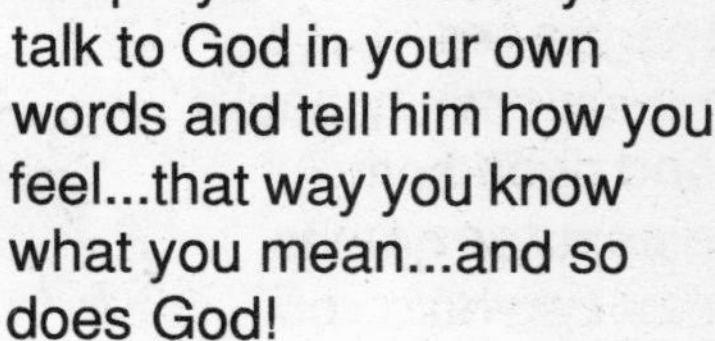

Admitting to God that you are sorry for your sins and want to live his way, means you are asking God to help you start a whole new way of life, as a follower of Jesus.

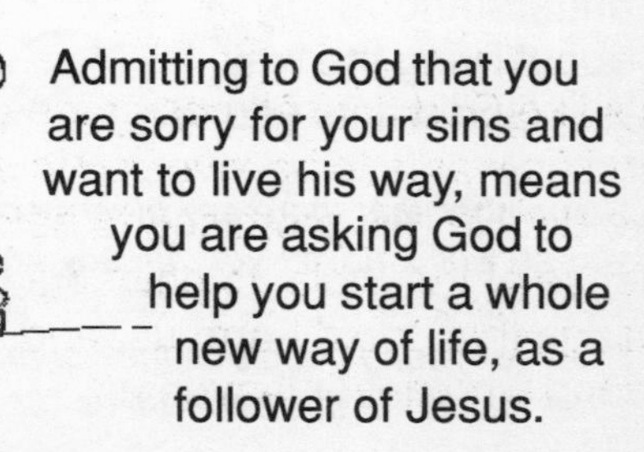

When we start listening to God, with the help of his Spirit, we try to stop doing, thinking and feeling wrong things, and begin to start thinking, feeling and doing what is right.

Now remember that it is a lifetime process and nobody is perfect. We may be tempted to go back to our old way of thinking, feeling and doing. Ask God to help you! Don't worry, God still loves you, forgives you and is still your friend.

To find out more about God and the life he wants for you, get a Bible. There are lots of different versions... even some for kids with nice easy words. There are also lots of videos of Bible stories, *books, magazines, CD's, tapes, activity packs and even some computer games that can help you understand more about living the way that God wants you to.

*Remember that there are other people who can help you as well...maybe you already know some people in local churches who could tell you about clubs or special times for young people at their church. * Look at the other section in this book Steps for new Christians*

Strong Medicine

Every bit of your body has its own special part to play in keeping you in good condition. If one part doesn't work, well then the whole body suffers.

A man in the Bible called Paul once described all the people who love God as a body...he asks us to think about some funny ideas he had.

He said, 'Imagine your whole body was made up of only one enormous eyeball! How could you smell things if this was the case?'

Paul was telling us that all the people who believe in Jesus need to act as if they are all a part of one body... everyone is important and has a special job to do to make sure that the whole body stays in shape!

This is good news for us, 'cause it means that we are all very special and have an important role to play.

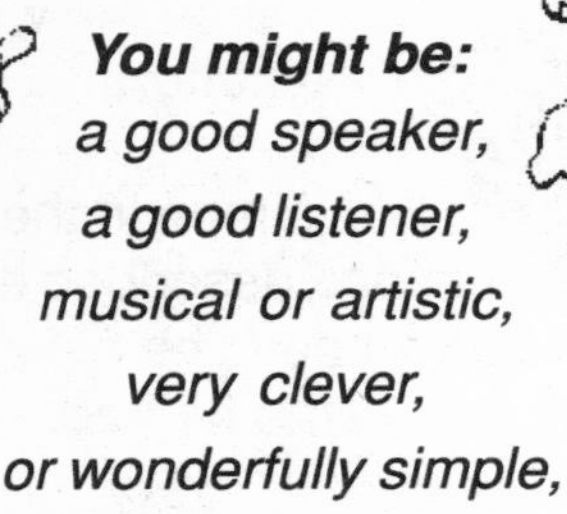

You might be:
a good speaker,
a good listener,
musical or artistic,
very clever,
or wonderfully simple,
good at making things
with your hands,
or solving problems
with your mind...

Whatever you can do, it's needed by someone else and God can use your particular function to help others!

People who are a part of this body are called the 'church' and the church is full of lots of different kinds of people.

When we start with the heart, and dedicate ourselves to Jesus, we find that the next thing that he wants us to do is to become dedicated to other people.

If our body is made up of all kinds of different people with different skills and talents then we should be able to help just about every kind of person in the world!

God really thinks about the best ways to help people! What are you good at? Are you working as well as you can or should be? If a body is to be strong and healthy then all its members and organs need to be working together properly.

Every part of this body is important to God, and important for other people...
You are a very important part of the church.

10 Body Building

We have discovered that we needed God's help to cure our sin. Now it's time to realise that we must have regular checkups to make sure that we remain healthy.

In the same way that someone recovering from an illness must be taken care of, so we need to look after our new life. The Bible tells us that there are some things that we need to do to stay in shape.

Reading the Bible is important because we find instructions on the best way to live, the kind of things to avoid and what we should be involved in. The Bible also gives us good examples of people who lived for God, and the kind of problems they overcame.

Praying is also important. It lets us speak to God about anything at all, we can thank him, say we are sorry, ask him to help us or others. Just as you talk freely with a friend, God wants you to speak openly to him.

Another important exercise is to ***meet together with others who love Jesus.***

This means that we can:
thank God together,
make friends,
talk about things that
we don't understand,
and help each other through
difficult times.

When people meet together, we usually call this 'church'. By reading, praying, listening, talking, thinking and living like Jesus did, we can become more and more like him.

Finally, the Bible tells us that it is important to ***let others know about Jesus*** in the things that we say and the things that we do.

You have some very good news for other people who don't know about sin and all that it can do. Don't be frightened to tell them and show them what Jesus has done for you, and what he can do for them. Introduce them to the best Doctor in the world! Jesus makes a special promise to all those that love him. Even though our human body eventually gets worn out, everyone who has faith in Jesus will be with him in heaven. What other doctor can say that?

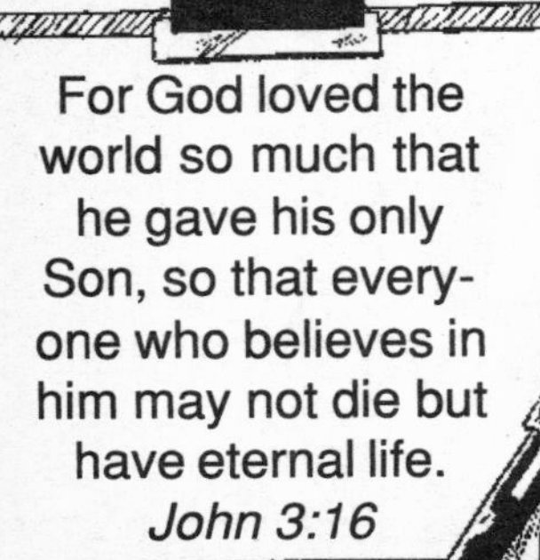

Steps for new Christians

So you've become a Christian!
There will be lots of things that you
will want to know about and understand,
and this little book is a great place to start!

Have a great time learning and
growing as a Christian...read on!

PS: If you don't understand some of the words that are used, remember to look at the back of the book for an explanation!

IT'S LIFE - BUT NOT AS WE KNOW IT

When you took the step of becoming a Christian, you started on a new way of life...living like Jesus!

Deciding to follow Jesus means that we have realised that we have been living the wrong way - our own way! Without God's love and forgiveness we cannot live as he intended us to.

Jesus loved his Father, and now that you have decided to follow him, your actions and thoughts towards God will also begin to change as you get to know him more.

Loving God with all that we have is the most important lesson that we can learn. But now that you are a Christian, you must also learn to love and care for others as well, (Jesus said that loving other people was the second most important thing that anyone can learn!).

Being a Christian means that you have started to have the best relationship that anyone could ever have!

THINK BEFORE YOU READ ON...

How did God begin to speak to you?

Was it through:

Maybe God began to show how much he cared for you by some other brilliant way?

God is not limited in how he speaks to us - it's important that we listen to what he says.

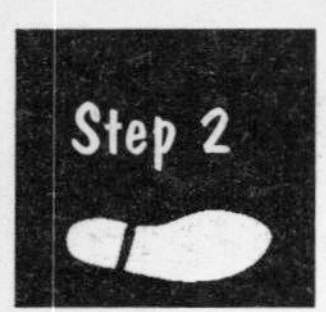

BABIES NEED FOOD

Just as your body needs food to keep it strong and healthy, so the new life you now have needs a good balanced diet. If you are going to grow into a strong Christian, you need to be fed!

God has given us a very special book, called the Bible which is full of good things which will help you to grow.

Milk is the food for babies. Did you know that some parts of the Bible are described as milk for new Christians? These are the best places to start reading.

GOOD FOOD FOR NEW CHRISTIANS

The Bible is a big book to read, so don't be put off by the size of it!

It begins with the story of God's amazing creation of the world. However, things go wrong when people start to disobey God and please themselves.

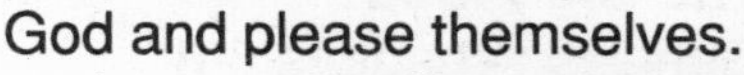

As a result, all people have been separated from God because of sin.

But it also tells us about God's great rescue plan. He has made it possible for everyone to become his friend if they want to - something you have just discovered!

The first part of the Bible is called the Old Testament and is actually made up of 39 separate 'books'. To begin your Bible adventure, turn over the page to find a good starting place...

SOME MILKY BITS...

Great stories which are easier to understand.

Where they're found in the Bible
(if you have difficulty finding these books, look up the contents page)

The Creation
Genesis : chapters 1-2

The Big Flood
Genesis : chapters 6-8

The Commands of God
Exodus : chapter 20 verses 1-17

The story of David
1 Samuel: chapters 16-31
2 Samuel: chapters 1-24

SOME MEATY BITS...

More great stories, which contain some harder bits to understand.

Joshua

The book of Joshua

Daniel
The book of Daniel

The books called:
Leviticus
Numbers
1 & 2 Chronicles

The second part of the Bible is called the New Testament and is made up of 27 books, (although some of them are actually short letters).

The New Testament talks a lot about a very special person - Jesus. The first 4 books are called the Gospels and they tell us who Jesus is, what he has done and what that means for us.

MILKY BITS

The stories about Jesus.
Stories that Jesus told.
Both found in the books:
Matthew, Mark, Luke and John.

The beginning of the book called Acts.

MEATY BITS

The book called **Romans**
The Book called **Hebrews**
The book called **James**

There are loads of other books in the Bible, these are just ideas to get you started.

As you start reading you'll soon see that there are some bits of the Bible that are more difficult to understand than others. As you 'grow up' you will be able to understand more of the meaty bits, but don't worry if it takes time! The important thing is to get the 'food' that you need.

As well as the Bible, you can get special videos, games, activity packs, CDs, tapes, stories and songs that will nourish you. Ask someone who has been a Christian for a while if they could find out about things that might help you! * *(See page 29 for more details)*

BABIES NEED A FAMILY

All babies need someone older to look after them. It is usually a family's job to take care of the newest member. Mum, dad, brothers, sisters granny,grandpa..... even aunts,uncles and cousins often help to look after a new arrival.

The Bible tells us that the people who are called the Church should be like a good family to us.

A church will be made up of old and young people, clever and not so clever. Tall, short, thin, not so thin, men, women, boys, girls, people who have white skin, people who have black skin, brown skin,cool clothes, scruffy clothes, people who can walk and people who can't: in fact, ***all kinds of people!***

What everyone of them should have in common is that they love Jesus and do their best to do what he says.

Remember though, just like any family, you may not always agree with everyone at church, and you can say 'No!' to anything that you think might be wrong.

Check first in the Bible to see if what people say or do matches up with the Bible's teaching. If you don't understand something then ask questions... If answers don't make sense to you then say so!

STEP 4

BABIES NEED CLEANED UP!

Babies make an awful mess! They spill things, they get food all over their faces and we won't go into the reason that they wear nappies!

Babies make silly mistakes all the time but it's the only way that they can grow and learn. Some mistakes are things that they cannot help, but they soon learn to stop doing those things.

Other mistakes are made because of bad behaviour. We all grow and learn by making mistakes but doing things wrong on purpose will stop us from growing up healthily. When we do make a mess, we need to learn to say sorry to God and to the people we've hurt.

BABIES HAVE THEIR OWN LANGUAGE

Parents love to hear their baby gurgle and laugh! It doesn't make any sense to anyone else, but it is the best sound in the world to a loving parent!

Talking to our heavenly Father is called prayer. You might have heard an older Christian praying and using very big strange words...don't worry! You don't need to talk like that.

God wants you to use your own words when you speak to him.

HOW DO I PRAY?

You can pray anywhere, anytime!

You can pray out loud or quietly, (God even knows what we think!).

You can thank God,

ask him to help you,

say you're sorry
for things you've done,

tell him
what makes you angry,
sad, happy or upset.

You can pray for others, but best of all,
the fact that we can pray means that we
can talk to God our friend!
God loves you, and sees you as a special,
valued, wonderful person...

God loves you!

THE TALK AND THE WALK

Jesus said that it was important to go and tell people the good news about what he wants to do for them. How do you think people might react if you start talking about your faith every time that you meet them?

Does what you say and what you do match up? If the most important thing is to love God first and then other people, are you showing that kind of love?

Will you continue to love someone even if they don't like what you believe...or even if they don't like you?

The Bible says that if we say that we believe in Jesus, but don't try to live like him, then it's like not having 'new life' at all. Jesus certainly told people about the love of God, but he also...well...check this out!

JESUS...

Spent time with children.

Treated women with great respect.

Allowed the sick to touch him.

Spent time with poor people.

Made friends
with people
who had no friends.

Was never horrible
to people because they
had a different religion,
looked different, or had
different coloured skin.

Spoke up for people
who found themselves
in trouble...

Jesus lived out everything that he believed...that's why they called him, 'The friend of sinners'.

It's important that you share your faith, but you have to show love and respect for other people, no matter how they might respond to what you have to say about Jesus.

YOU'RE NEVER ALONE WHEN YOU'RE ON YOUR OWN

Even when we are on our own, we need to remember that God is still with us. If we are sad or happy, lonely or feeling misunderstood, God has promised to be with us at all times!

If your friends or family make fun of you for becoming a Christian, remember you're not alone - Jesus knew what it felt like to have a hard time.

When doubts or fears try to destroy your new joy and faith, take some of God's promises to heart.

Check out some of the things that he has said...

Although we can't see Jesus here with us, he promised that he would send his Holy Spirit to be our helper. When we ask Jesus to forgive us and take control of our lives, it is the Holy Spirit who comes and lives inside us.

This promise is amazing! It means that we don't have to count on how we *feel*, but can rely on God's faithfulness.

STEP 8

UNDER PRESSURE...

It was the summer holidays and Harry, Yuk and Snot went *every-where* together, they were closer than a goldfish's eyes!

Yuk was called Yuk because, apart from burgers, fries and sweet things, he hated any other kind of food.

'Fancy some soup?' his mum would say.

'Yuk!' said Yuk.

'How about some nice chicken curry?'

'Yuk!'

'Stew?'

'Yuk!'...and so on! Harry thought that Yuk was cool. 'I wish I could be like Yuk,' he thought.

Snot was completely different from Yuk! Some people thought that he was called Snot because he never carried a hanky, but that was only part of the reason! Snot always thought that *he* knew what was best. If mum told him that it was long past his bed time, Snot would say, 'S'not!'

Harry thought that Snot was excellent, 'I wish I was as smart as Snot!' he thought.

Harry was called Harry because he was called Harry. Harry usually ate all his meals, and went to bed when he was asked to, but he felt like he was really ordinary...nothing special...a bit boring...well, he didn't even have a cool name like Snot!

PRESSURE...PRESSURE...

Yuk always got the best kind of trainers to wear, but Harry had to make do with cheaper ones, just because his dad didn't have a job.

Snot didn't even have a dad, but he still wore better trainers than Harry, and worst of all, sometimes Yuk and Snot would joke about Harry's affordable footwear!

'Right! That's it!', thought Harry, 'if Snot and Yuk can have cool names so can I! If Yuk and Snot can get good trainers, so can I! No one's gonna joke about me anymore...first I need a name!'

Harry thought for ages, 'I've got it ,'Bogie,' Naaa! Too much like Snot! Hmmm...what about 'Belch' or, 'Ugh!' Wait a minute...I've got it...'Finknot'...that's it, I am gonna be Finknot!'

The first job was to get rid of the terrible trainers; it was time to have a word with Mum and Dad!

Harry picked up the sports shoes and headed off to the living room.

'Hi Harry! What are you up to ?' yelled Dad.

'Don't call me Harry!' said Harry, 'everyone calls me Finknot.'

'Finknot...since when?' asked Mum.

'Ummm...For a while now, anyway never mind that, just look at these trainers!'

Harry's mum and dad looked.

'What about them?' said Dad.

'Are they letting water in?' whined Mum.

Harry's face went pink. 'No!' He yelled, 'Look at them...just look at them!'

UNDER PRESSURE...

Both parents looked. Harry could feel himself getting more and more frustrated.

'You just don't get it do you! Who has ever heard of 'Kiddywinkle' trainers...it's the name... I don't want to wear 'Kiddywinkle' trainers!'

'Well then what *do* you want?' both parents asked in stereo.

'I want Super Pumperama Lazerdisc Urban Street Feet Trainers!'

Harry could see that Mum looked sad. 'We can't afford those kind of shoes Harry. I'm sorry, but you will just need to wear the ones that you have for the time being.'

Harry got ready to use his new name.

'I Finknot!' he yapped, 'you will just need to get me the ones that I want...or else!'

'Yes!' said Dad, 'Or else change your name to 'Finkagain'.'

Mum giggled. Harry didn't. For days Harry grumped around the house, only speaking to his mum and dad when he really had to. 'I'll teach 'em' he thought.

'Tomato soup for lunch!' shouted Dad.

'Finknot!' said Harry who would not touch a drop!

'It's bed time !' cried Mum.

'Finknot' growled Harry as he kept reading his comics.

PRESSURE...PRESSURE...

For days it went on but Harry was *not* going to leave the house in those trainers. After a whole week, Harry was miserable. 'Alright Harry, let's get this sorted out once and for all!' said Dad.

'Finknot!' said Harry quietly.

'Finkagain!' said Dad. This time no one giggled! 'You need to tell me why you are behaving this way Harry. It's causing problems for everyone, not just you!' Harry frowned.

'Why can't I have the new trainers? They don't cost all that much, and you can always afford to put money into the church's collection plate and stuff like that!'

'So that's it!' said Dad. 'Harry you need to understand that Mum and I need to use our money in the best way that we can. We need to pay for our house, our fuel bills, our food, and our clothes. The money we give to church is just as important as any of the other things that we do!'

'Why?' said Harry, 'church is just boring!' Dad sat down on the edge of Harry's bed.

'The little bit of money we give to the church is used in all kinds of different ways. There are practical things needing to be paid for, like heating the building, so that you and I don't freeze on Sunday mornings! How do you think all the games for your club are paid for? The church also helps to send people to work with children who have much less than us!'

Harry's eyes widened, 'You mean there are other kids who have worse trainers than me?'

His dad smiled, but still looked serious. 'Harry,

some children have no parents, no home, no medicine, no food and even no clean water!'

Harry felt bad! Still, what was he going to do? He couldn't back down and he still wanted to have a cool name. Just as his dad left the room, Harry had a brainwave. He got his brightest coloured model paints and painted a big blue line right across the word 'Kiddywinkle'. It looked neat! A red squiggle, a green circle and a big yellow star began to appear on the hated trainers! Within an hour the shoes where dry and on Harry's feet and were carrying him right down to Snot's house.

Snot's mum opened the door.

'Hello Harry!' she smiled. 'Haven't seen you for a while.'

Just then Snot and Yuk came bounding down the stairs...both of them stared at Harry's wildly coloured shoes.

'Where did you get those trainers?' they both yelled.

'Yeah', continued Snot, 'They're cooler than a penguin's bottom!'

'Wish I had a pair' said Yuk, 'how come you always manage to be different Harry?'

'The name is Finkabout!' said Harry.

PRESSURE...PRESSURE...

'Finkabout!' squealed his mates, 'why Finkabout?'

Harry smiled, 'Because from today, I began to Finkabout how special I am and all the things that I have. I realised that trying to be like you guys just makes me miserable, because I'm different. I've had to Finkabout others who don't have nearly as much as me, and that made me Finkabout how selfish I can be. The most important thing I've had to Finkabout is that people need to see the real me! I'm not going to try to be like you Snot, or you Yuk...that just makes everybody miserable!'

The three pals wandered off towards the park laughing and joking.

Finkabout was first to run for the old swings,and just before Snot and Yuk followed, Snot whispered, 'I wish I was as smart as Harry!'

'Yeah!' said Yuk, 'and I wish that I could have cool trainers like his, I mean just look at these old things I've got...Yuk!

UNDER PRESSURE...

It can be hard to feel happy with the way that we are. Sometimes our friends put us under pressure to do and say things that we wouldn't normally do. It's possible that sometimes they don't even mean it! But it is important that we know when we are being pressurised.

If you are asked to do something which is wrong, have the guts to say 'No!' Remember, you can pray for help at any time!

The Bible tells us that we need to learn to be content with the good things that we already have. Wanting what other people have usually makes us want even more!

FRUIT - NOT SOUR GRAPES!

It's a well known fact that fruit is good for you! Fruit is the proof that a tree or a plant is strong and healthy.

The Bible tells us that a growing Christian should also have proof that he or she is healthy in their faith! Yep! We need to bear fruit! Don't panic...you don't need to have bananas growing out of your nose.

Just as milk was a way to describe the simple, but important parts of the Bible, so fruit has another meaning!

The Bible tells us that the fruit that we bear shows others that we are living like Jesus...it is proof that we have the new life that he promised us! Are you an impatient person normally? Well, the Bible says that *patience* is some of the fruit that a Christian should have!

Are there people that you really hate? The fruit of this new life should be replacing that hate with love!

In the Bible in the book called Galatians, chapter 5, verses 22 and 23 you will find there are 9 fruits mentioned. These are all called the fruit of the Spirit, which means that we are showing qualities as a result of the Holy Spirit living within us.

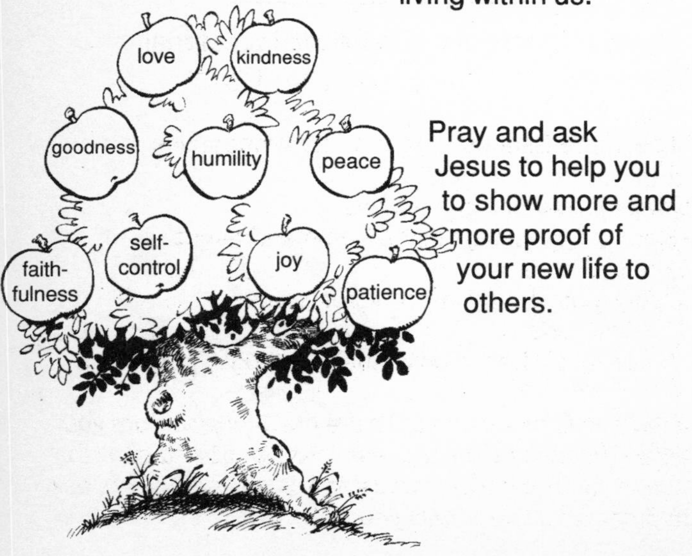

Pray and ask Jesus to help you to show more and more proof of your new life to others.

FOREVER FRIENDS

God has promised to always be our closest friend... absolutely nothing can change that!

He will always love us and never leave us. Even when our bodies die, our friendship with God will not end. He promises us that he will have a special place, called Heaven for us to go to, and we will be with him forever.

You may find the following material will help you to grow up...

MUSIC: by Sammy Horner & The Wonderkids

Obey the Maker's Instructions
- Rock n' Roll version of the Commandments.
Country Parables
-Country music version of Jesus' stories
The Beatitudes
- Blues music based on Jesus' teaching in Matthew 5

If the above tapes and CD's are not available from your local Christian bookshop, ask them to order a copy for you. If you are unsure where to find the bookshop, ask another Christian to help you.

PARDON ME?

As you grow up in your faith you may come across strange new words and ideas. To help you understand them we've tried to explain them...

BIBLE - The special book that God has given us. He told lots of people who believed in him to write down, laws, stories, the words of Jesus and the story about how the Church began. The Bible tells us what we need to know about men and women, God, Jesus, how we should live, looking after the planet, caring for others and more. It is called God's Word or Scripture.

BORN AGAIN- When we decide to follow Jesus he promises us a new life. The beginning of that new life is like being born again. A chance to start again and have a whole new way of thinking and living...but it's just the start!

CHRISTIAN- Any person of any age who loves Jesus and obeys what Jesus taught.

CHURCH-The name given to all the people who believe in Jesus no matter where they might live in the world.

CREATOR - A name for God, 'cos he made everything!

FAITH- Being able to believe in God without actually having seen him! It can also mean what we believe as Christians.

FRUIT- Proof that we are living like Jesus.

GOD - God is everywhere, and he knows everything and sees everything. God is Love, God is good, he is fair, and the most powerful person anywhere!

GOSPEL - This is the Good News about Jesus and every thing that he has done for us and all that he wants to do for us, and how we can get involved.

HEAVEN - A special place that God has made. When our bodies die, we will go there to be with God forever. Heaven is a wonderful place where people won't be sad or unhappy.

HEAVENLY FATHER - A name for God. Jesus tells us that our Heavenly Father is always good to us and knows what we need, so no matter how good or bad our normal dad might be, God is always even better.

JESUS - This is the name that was given to God's Son. Jesus means 'Saviour'. Jesus is God in human form.

LORD - Another name for Jesus. The Lord is someone who is in control of everything, and is wise and fair.

LOVE - Love doesn't just mean that you go all silly every time you see that cute girl or handsome boy in your class. The Bible says that God is Love! God's love is limitless. He loves people no matter how rotten they might be.

MILK - The important things that we need to know about our faith, that are simple to understand when a new Christian.

NEW LIFE - What you have after you are born again!

PRAYER - Talking with God about anything at all!

SINNER - The bible says that *every* person who ever lived is a sinner, (except Jesus). We sin when we disobey God.

SPEAK - When we talk about God 'speaking' to us we mean that we have read the Bible and understood what God wants us to do. God also reminds you of things that are wrong or need changed by showing you things on TV, in books or magazines or by what someone might say to you.

SPIRIT - The Holy Spirit is God, and he came to us after Jesus went to heaven. He gives us our new life and helps us understand what he wants us to do for him.

It's exciting to see a baby take their first few steps. Steps lead on to walking,jumping, running...action!

Growing involves learning new things, taking risks and being able to change your mind. God wants his children to grow up to be strong and useful and to love him. Keep growing!

Good books with the real message of hope!

Christian Focus Publications publishes biblically-accurate books for adults and children.

If you are looking for quality Bible teaching for children then we have a wide and excellent range of Bible story books - from board books to teenage fiction, we have it covered.

You can also try our new Bible teaching Syllabus for 3-9 year olds and teaching materials for pre-school children.

These children's books are bright, fun and full of biblical truth, an ideal way to help children discover Jesus Christ for themselves. Our aim is to help children find out about God and get them enthusiastic about reading the Bible, now and later in their lives.

Find us at our web page:
www.christianfocus.com